for Fabian

First published in the United States 1990 by

Atomium Books Inc.
Suite 300
1013 Centre Road
Wilmington, DE 19805.

First edition published in German, by K. Thienemanns Verlag, Stuttgart-Wien, 1989
under the title "Die Wolkenreise".
Text and pictures copyright © K. Thienemanns Verlag 1989.
English translation copyright © Atomium Books 1990.

Printed and bound in Belgium by
Color Print Graphix, Antwerp.
First U.S. Edition
ISBN 1-56182-021-0
2 4 6 8 10 9 7 5 3 1

The Cloud's Journey

Illustrations by Sis Koch
Story by Sigrid Heuck
English text adapted by Philomena Korbutt

atomium books

Once the wind met a small cloud.
It was white, soft and airy
— as clouds are.

The wind saw that this cloud
could float through the sky with ease.
So the wind called to the small cloud,
"Let me carry you on an exciting journey!
I can show you a whole new world from up here!"

I will show you lush forests,

fields filled with flowers and waving wheat,

rolling hills with wild horses

and herds of cattle.

I will show you enchanted cities filled with skyscrapers,

lonely deserts — covered in silence,

towering mountains and steep, rocky shores.

I will show you magical ships,

fabulous fish swimming through coral reefs,
smoking volcanoes,
and much, much more . . .

You and I could explore together
if only you'd let me carry you
all around this wonderful world.

To the small cloud
it sounded like a fascinating adventure.

It thought carefully, then sadly called,
"I would love to join you on your journey,
but I cannot go with you today.
The sky is beginning to darken . . .

. . . and I promised I would rain.

Maybe we could go another day?"